D1500955

This book belongs to

. . . .

Written & Illustrated
By
Lesley D. Nurse

ISBN# 978-0-9797699-6-2

Table of Contents

Always dream.

Once upon a time,
there was once a
little girl named Reeby.

She was everyone's
friend and the
apple of her family's eye.

Reeby was very charming and smart and it was very easy for her to get anything she wanted.

It was the day of Reeby's birthday and she couldn't wait to celebrate with her friends after recess.

To her surprise,
Reeby's mother approached her
in the playground
with a beautiful pink box.

She opened it up and
it was a sparkling tiara.
This was the perfect gift
for such a special day.

" Today is my birthday and it's all about me today!" she cheerfully gushed out.

" Now, now Reeby,
we talked about this,"
her mother forewarned
before continuing,
" It's your birthday,
but don't let it get to
your head."

With a look of gloom,
Reeby pouted her lips
and folded her arms in protest
to what her mother advised.

As soon as Reeby re-entered school, she let go of her mother's hand to dash for her classroom.

She yelled for her mother
to hurry. Once Reeby
got to her classroom door,
she panicked at the sight of the
dark room and quietness.

" Mommy! Where is everyone?
No one is here to celebrate
my birthday!"

" I don't know Reeby. Lets go inside and see what happened," she calmly suggested.

Slowly, Reeby opened the door with her head tilted down in sadness.

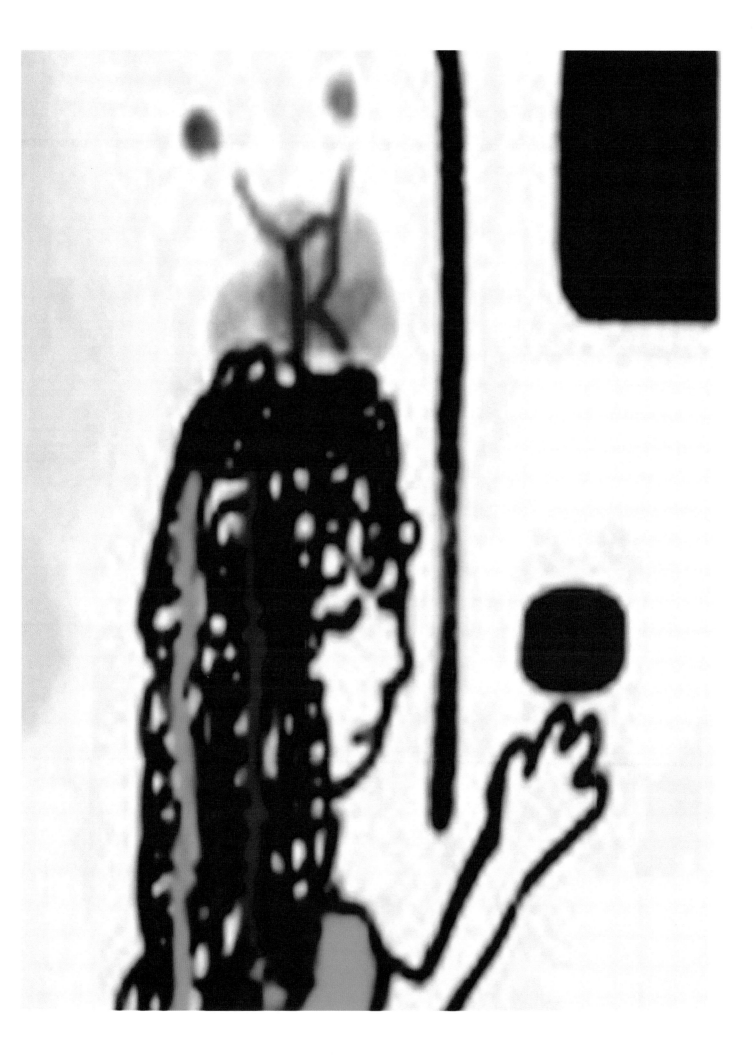

Suddenly she saw a spark and it was a beautiful cake with beaming lit candles, with all of her friends standing by smiling.

" Surprise!" they shouted as the lights were turned on.

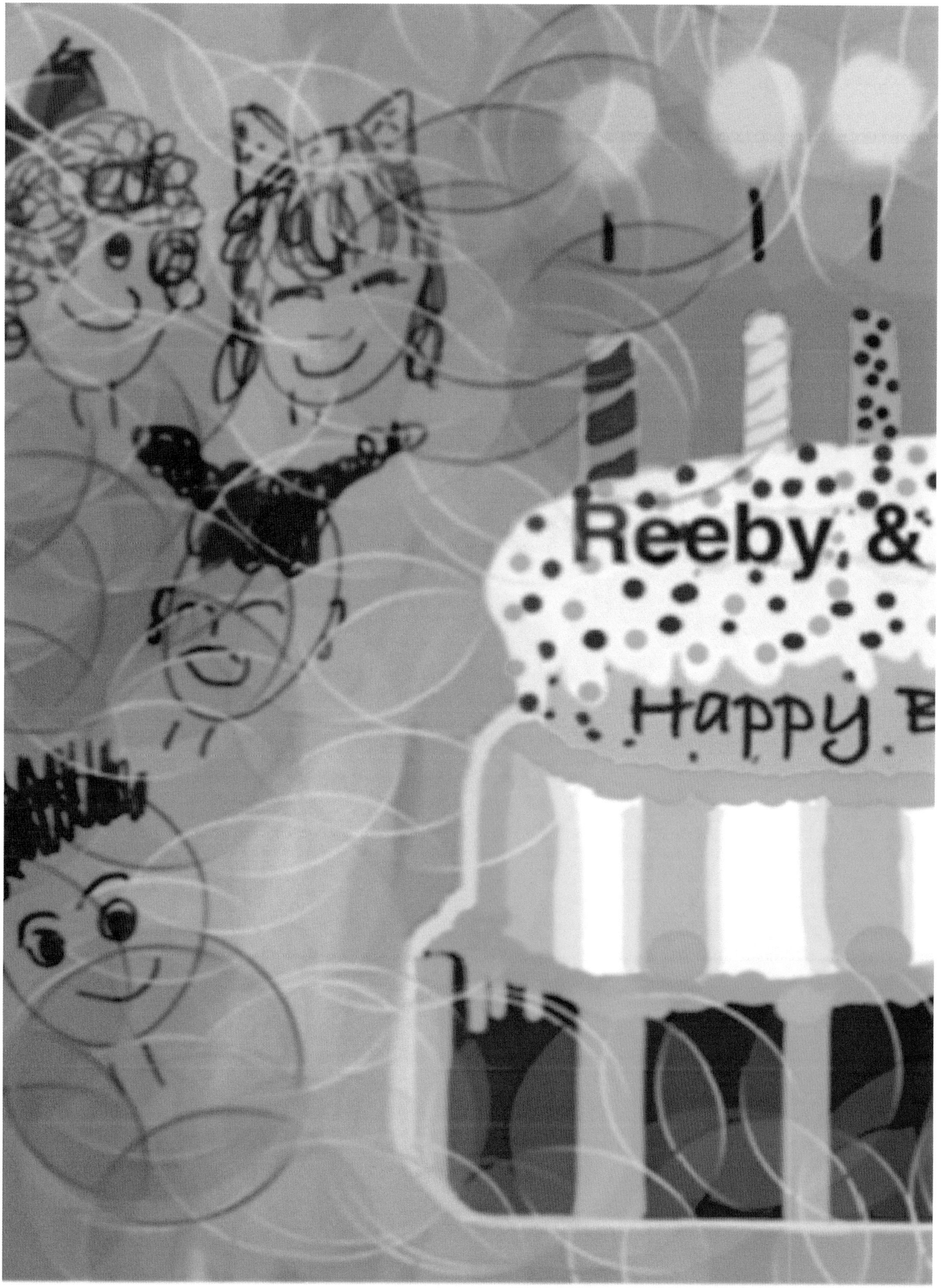
Reeby &
Happy B

" For me?" she asked bashfully.
All of her friends were
elbow to elbow
with hugs and kisses.

" See mommy, it is all about me!" she boasted.

" Time to cut the cake
Reeby!" said her teacher.
Reeby was more than ready
to cut the cake for her
very special day.

She straightened out her back and proudly flashed her classmates her winning smile.

Reeby kept blowing kisses
and winks when
suddenly, she heard her
teacher call out another name.
" Come on up S-p-e-n-c-e-r!"

Reeby was not happy
that the cake read
Reeby and Spencer.

Reeby & Spencer

Happy Birthday

" What?! This is my birthday! Why do I have to share on my day!" she yelled.

Reeby ran towards the back of the classroom and kneeled down in the corner and burst into tears.

Everyone was at a loss
for words and didn't
know what to do.

Then Reeby cried in her
mother's arms and asked,
" why would this horrible
thing happen to me
on my day?"

" Reeby, it's true that today is your birthday; but you also share this day with Spencer as well. It's not just about you sweetheart, it's about Spencer too."

As Reeby's head nestled in her mother's arms, she had a moment of clarity. "Mommy, if I share does that mean that I have something in common with Spencer?"

" Yes it does Reeby and you'll also have a friend."

" I want to be friends!"

" I'm ready to cut my,
I mean our cake now!"
Reeby said before
returning to her
birthday party.

While scurrying to return to her party, Reeby could see her classmates laughing and eating cake.

She quickly made her way
back to the front
of the classroom for
a piece of cake;
but it was all gone.

She began to feel sad again
and left out of
her birthday party.

Then Reeby felt a tap
on her shoulder.

" Want some cake Reeby?"
asked Spencer.

"Yup, I sure do!"

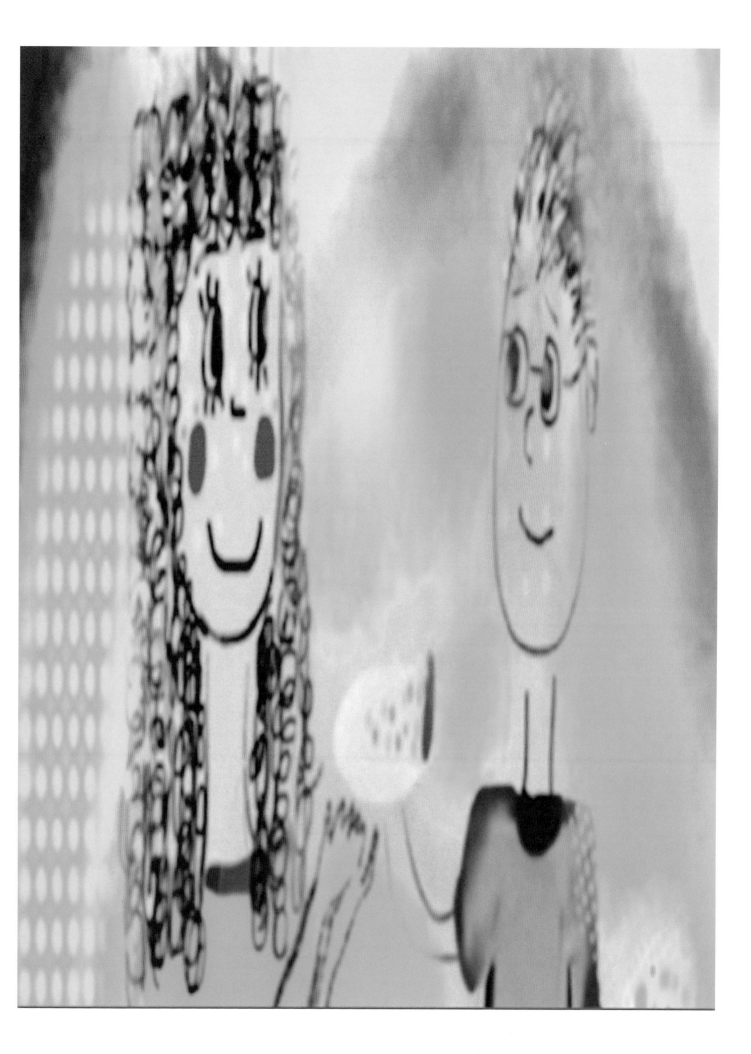

The End

Dictionary

Bashfully
reluctant to draw attention to oneself; shy.

Boasted
brag, crow, swagger, swank, gloat, show off.

Celebrate
publicly acknowledge (a significant or happy
day or event) with a social gathering or
enjoyable activity.

Charming
pleasant or attractive.

Clarity
the quality of being clear, in particular.

Forewarned
warn, warn in advance, give advance warning,
give fair warning, give notice.

Horrible
causing or likely to cause horror; shocking, .

Nestled
settle or lie comfortably within or against
something.

Panicked
sudden uncontrollable fear or anxiety.

Scurrying
move hurriedly with short quick
steps;run,dash.

Suddenly
quickly and unexpectedly.

Suggested
put forward for consideration.

www.greedyreeby.com
Also available on Amazon.com
contact@thetaleofgreedyreeby.com
Like "Greedy Reeby" on Facebook
Follow "Greedy Reeby" on Twitter

Made in the USA
Charleston, SC
01 July 2014